S0-AXD-685

I'm going to read

I'm Going To READ!™

These levels are meant only as guides;
you and your child can best choose a book that's right.

Level 1: Kindergarten–Grade 1 . . . Ages 4–6
- word bank to highlight new words
- consistent placement of text to promote readability
- easy words and phrases
- simple sentences build to make simple stories
- art and design help new readers decode text

Level 2: Grade 1 . . . Ages 6–7
- word bank to highlight new words
- rhyming texts introduced
- more difficult words, but vocabulary is still limited
- longer sentences and longer stories
- designed for easy readability

Level 3: Grade 2 . . . Ages 7–8
- richer vocabulary of up to 200 different words
- varied sentence structure
- high-interest stories with longer plots
- designed to promote independent reading

Level 4: Grades 3 and up . . . Ages 8 and up
- richer vocabulary of more than 300 different words
- short chapters, multiple stories, or poems
- more complex plots for the newly independent reader
- emphasis on reading for meaning

Note to Parents

What a great sense of achievement it is when you can accomplish a goal! With the **I'm Going To Read!**™ series, goals are established when you pick up a book. This series was developed to grow with the new reader. The vocabulary grows quantifiably from 50 different words at Level One, to 100 different words at Level Two, to 200 different words at Level Three, and to 300 different words at Level Four.

Ways to Use the Word Bank

- Read along with your child and help him or her sound out the words in the word bank.

- Have your child find the word in the word bank as you read it aloud.

- Ask your child to find the word in the word bank that matches a picture on the page.

- Review the words in the word bank and then ask your child to read the story to you.

Related Word Bank Activities

- Create mini-flash cards in your handwriting. This provides yet another opportunity for the reader to be able to identify words, regardless of what the typography looks like.

- Think of a sentence and then place the mini-flash cards on a table out of order. Ask your child to rearrange the mini-flash cards until the sentence makes sense.

- Make up riddles about words in the story and have your child find the appropriate mini-flash card. For example, "It's red and it bounces. What is it?"

- Choose one of the mini-flash cards and ask your child to find the same word in the text of the story.

- Create a second set of mini-flash cards and play a game of Concentration, trying to match the pairs of words.

LEVEL 1

STERLING CHILDREN'S BOOKS
New York

An Imprint of Sterling Publishing Co., Inc.
1166 Avenue of the Americas
New York, NY 10036

Lot: 16 18 20 19 17 15 02/17

Published by Sterling Publishing Co., Inc.
Text © 2005 by Harriet Ziefert Inc.
Illustrations © 2005 by R.W. Alley
Distributed in Canada by Sterling Publishing
c/o Canadian Manda Group, 664 Annette Street,
Toronto, Ontario, Canada M6S 2C8
Distributed in the United Kingdom by GMC Distribution Services,
Castle Place, 166 High Street, Lewes, East Sussex, England BN7 1XU
Distributed in Australia by NewSouth Books 45 Beach Street,
Coogee, NSW 2034, Australia

I'm Going To Read is a trademark of Sterling Publishing Co., Inc.

Manufactured in China
All rights reserved

ISBN: 978-1-4027-2721-4

For information about custom editions, special sales, premium and
corporate purchases, please contact Sterling Special Sales
Department at 800-805-5489 or specialsales@sterlingpublishing.com.

The Prince's Tooth Is Loose!

Pictures by R. W. Alley

STERLING CHILDREN'S BOOKS
New York

A little prince
went on a picnic.

The little prince
would not eat.

"My tooth is loose!" he cried.
"I cannot eat!"

"The prince's tooth is loose!"
cried the nanny.

"He cannot eat!
He cannot eat!"

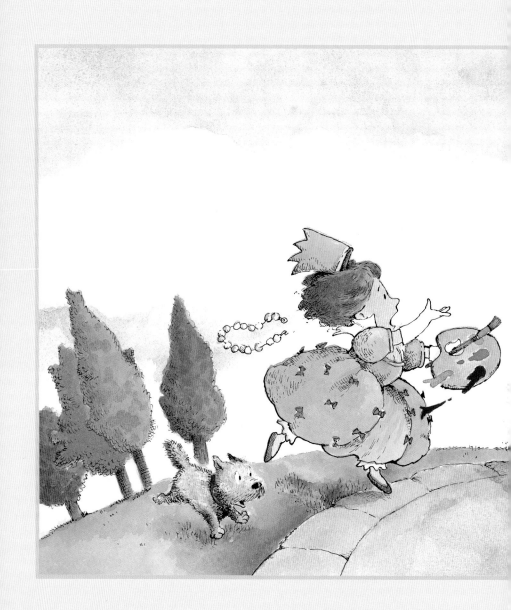

"The tooth must come out!"
said the queen.

"I'll call the general!"
said the king.

"The tooth must come out!"
said the king.
"Find the nearest apple."

"I'll find one!"
said the general.

The general called his men.

"Find the nearest apple!"
he cried.

The men found lots of apples.

The general
gave an apple
to the king.

The king gave it
to the queen.

The queen
gave the apple
to the nanny.

The nanny gave it
to the little prince.

The little prince
bit into the apple . . .

**and his tooth
fell out!**

"Now find the
nearest tooth fairy!"
said the little prince.

THE END